That Is Where Home Is

EILEEN DISTASIO-CLARK

With Great Love and Appreciation to those who Have and Do Bless My Life

My Family:

Joseph DeStasio Sr. & Miriam Lucille Baragone DeStasio, My Late Parents.

Andrea Jean DeStasio McIntosh, My Older Sister and their Family.

Joseph DeStasio Jr., My Younger and Only Brother and their Family.

Donna Marie DeStasio Wagner, My Younger Sister and their Family.

My Children:

Eileen, Rebekah, Rachel, S. Michael,

Jennifer, Sharon, Tara, Stephanie,

Apryll, Mikaelah, & M. Trevor

and THEIR Families!!

ACKNOWLEDGMENTS

First and foremost, I express, deeply, my sincere gratitude to our Heavenly Father for blessing me with the gift and talent of writing! I know I could not do what I do without His assistance.

I also want to acknowledge and express gratitude to the members of my birth family—Joseph Sr., Miriam, Andrea, Joseph Junior, and Donna. All the experiences of my childhood years, experiences that taught me so very much and enabled me to reveal my true self to myself, came about through my experiences and relationships with them.

And, of course, it goes without saying, but I will say it anyway: I also want to acknowledge and note my gratitude to my children, Eileen, Rebekah, Rachel, S. Michael, Jennifer, Sharon, Tara, Stephanie, Apryll, Mikaelah, and M. Trevor, and their families! Through multiple things they said to me, over multiple years, I finally came to the realization that Heavenly Father gave me the gift of writing and opened the doors to these experiences because He knew that by sharing them with others, others could feel His love too.

And He definitely wants us all to know that He, Heavenly Father, Heavenly Mother, and Jehovah truly do loves us!!!

INTRODUCTION

There are sixteen books in this series, which I refer to as *"The Ellie Series."* All of the characters in these stories portray real people from my life. The main characters depict the members of my family: Daddy is my daddy; Mommy is my mommy; Jeannie is my older sister; Junior is my brother; Maria is my younger sister; and Ellie is me. Now, those are not our actual first names, but they do reference us.

The first story in the series presents our Heavenly Father's Plan of Salvation and takes place in the Pre-Earth World. Now, of course, because we all—when we were born—received what is known as The Veil of Forgetfulness, I do not actually remember everything from or about the Pre-Earth World, but I do know about and understand it from much study and worship as a member of The Church of Jesus Christ of Latter-Day Saints, and memories restored to me through the Holy Spirit. So, from this story there is much truth to be learned.

The last story in the series is set in the Post-Mortal World, and presents a depiction of what happens to us after this life. Again, because I have not gone there yet, I cannot say I 'remember' this. But, I have also learned about the Post-Mortal World from much study and worship as a member of The Church of Jesus Christ of Latter-Day Saints.

All of the other stories are based on true events from my life; events that actually occurred when and how they are depicted in these stories. I chose these events because they are among the many occurrences in my life that presented, or revealed that which I already knew without having to be taught, Principles of Eternal Truths.

Also, I chose these events as the settings for my stories because they depict wonderful learning moments from my childhood and adolescent years, lessons that have blessed and benefited me throughout the whole of my life and will forever continue to do so. Also, through these great truths and their consequences in my life, I have been able to share them with many others, whose lives have also been blessed by them.

So, please read and enjoy, then care and share the messages and stories with others!!

Now, there are also a couple of things you can look for:

In each story, the title of the previous story is presented in *italicized* form, the title of the next story is presented in *Capitalized Italicized* form, and the title of the story being read is presented in **emboldened** form.

Also, every story has at least one word that is uncommon or 'created.'

So, as you read, search, find, and have fun!

THAT IS WHERE HOME IS

It had been a long day and Ellie was more than ready for bed, which was something quite unusual for her. Remember, Ellie never was a good sleeper, not as a baby, not as a toddler or a little child, not as a teenager, and not even as an adult. Nope, Ellie never slept well, so she also never was ready for bed. But that day, Ellie had been quite busy getting everything ready for tomorrow, the day that she and her parents would be going to Kensington, Maryland, so that night, she really was ready for bed.

'Hold on!' You may be thinking, 'Why were they going there?' You may also be wondering, 'And why would it have taken Ellie all day to get ready?'

Well, just because I think you are thinking and wondering those thoughts, I will tell you why. It was the 7th of July, 1977, two days before Ellie and her fiancé were going to be married and sealed in the Washington D.C. Temple. Because everyone had to be at the temple quite early on the 9th of July, they decided to go down to Kensington one day before the wedding, on the 8th of July. So, on that day, the 7th of July, Ellie had been very busy getting ready everything she needed for her wedding, as well as the trip itself. That is why it took her all day. After all, there had been quite a lot to do! But now, she was done, and because it was so late, she was also ready for bed.

***Side Note:** While Ellie was ready for bed, and slept pretty well, she actually woke up earlier than she usually did. And because I am assuming that you are asking why, I will tell you.

She had had a very unusual dream, and when she awoke from the dream, she simply could not get it out of her thoughts. In fact, she really did not even want to do so, because it had been a very interesting dream. So, she just laid in bed pondering...

Wait! I have an idea. We can just join her in her thoughts so you can see her dream. Do you want to do that? You do?! Good!! Then let us be going.

Orsea stood quietly, a bit of a distance from all the others who were present, watching the procession that led to the Judgement Bar of God. When each person approached that bar, Jehovah, with His apostles, went over the records of their lives, the records that had been recorded and kept on earth, and the records that had been recorded in the Book of Life, which was kept in Heaven.

But there was also another record by which they were judged, a record they most definitely could not challenge because they, themselves, had kept that record. What, perhaps, most people never understood was that no one ever truly forgot anything. Every thought they ever thought, every word they ever spoke, every attitude they ever displayed, every action they ever enacted... everything that had been a part of their lives was stored in the tablets of their mind. So, whether or not a person could recall a memory while on Areth, it was there, saved permanently, in its full accurateness, to come forth on their judgement day, either to testify for them in their favor, or to testify against them to their demise. And they would be the ones who would speak the words of all that was recorded in their minds. So, quite honestly, in the 'courtroom of heaven,' they, we all, are our own witnesses, jurors, and judges!

Once the readings and their personal testimonies were completed, their Final Judgement was announced. When it was, some of them were filled with great joy at the pronouncement of their eternal fate, for they had done very well during the years of their mortal life, making right choices, and amending wrong ones, accepting Heavenly Father's one true gospel as their roadmap through their journey of mortal life, and making and keeping the covenants that were a part of that gospel.

But for others, the joy was not that great. Yes, they had done well, but not well enough to receive all that they could have obtained, for either they had not accepted the Father's plan while on Areth or, if they had, they had not lived it valiantly. Instead, they had made too many compromises, picking and choosing what they would follow and what they would ignore, how well they would adhere to the principles of the gospel, or how much they would amend them for their own comfort and liking. So, while they could still receive pleasant glory, they could not receive all that there was to receive.

And then, even more sadly, there were many, far too many, who were receiving their eternal fate with great sorrow, for they had not done well. Not only had they not accepted the Father's Plan of Salvation as their guidebook through mortality, they had willfully made wrong choices—choices they knew were wrong—but they did not care. And because they did not care, they did not amend those errors so that they could gain nothing more than the least degree of glory!

Now, most heart-wrenching of all were those who earned no glory. They could not, because not only had they chosen to not live according to Father's plan, they chose to turn against Father and follow Lucifer, doing as he did. So, all they could receive was darkness.

As Ellie watched her brothers and sisters advance to the Judgement Bar, receive the appropriate judgement, according to how they had chosen to live their mortal lives, and then go on to the kingdom, or darkness, to which they had been assigned. She could see that they all knew, every one of them, that the judgement they received was final and fair. There could be no going back to do it over. It was done! And it was justified!

"Where is your smile, Orsea," came a voice from behind her.

Turning to see, who she knew that it was, Orsea, in a whimsical tone, replied, "Well, Adlor, I guess I forgot to get it out of my pocket."

After they both chuckled a bit, Adlor, knowing what Orsea was thinking, said softly and lovingly, "Orsea, I knew you would have a difficult time seeing the sorrow on the faces of all those who lost what we all said we wanted, but I also know that you knew this would happen."

"Yes, Adlor," Orsea confirmed, "I do know, and always have, that we are the ones who, by our own choices; right and wrong, by our own actions; good or not good, and by our own responses to all of our choices and actions, words and thoughts, attitudes and... well, you know what I am saying. We are the ones who determined what we would or would not receive, for all eternity.

"And, Adlor, worry not. I know that it is just. If our Parents tried to give us more than we earned, more than we became able to receive, it would not be to our glory, it would be to our demise. They can only give us what we prepared ourselves to be able to endure and worthy to receive.

"And really, Adlor, I am okay with that. What makes me a little bit sad, though, is knowing that every one of us, even those who obtained less than the best, less than the highest kingdom and glory, could have received it all, if only they had done what they could have done instead of just what they did do."

Taking Orsea's hand in his, Adlor said, with compassion, "You are so loving and caring, Orsea. I know, in fact, we all know that you would do anything that you could, to help everyone that you could help, in every way that help would be needed. I am so proud of you."

"Oh, Adlor," Orsea responded in a tone of complete gratitude, "thank you. That means a lot to me, especially coming from you! You see, I know why you were chosen to be one of Father's prophets in the Latter Days, and I know that your life was not easy. You always have been a wonderfully valiant brother and you have learned and grown ever so much more. So, I really do know that you fully understand not just what I feel but why I feel it. And that makes me so very happy!"

"Good! Happy is what I want you always to be!" Adlor said sweetly. Then, before leaving her side to go attend to a task that had been assigned to him, he added, "Now, the first time I saw you on Areth, at the Hill Cumorah Pageant, you were wearing a sweet, loving smile, like the one in your pocket. So, I want you to get that smile out of your pocket and put it where it belongs, on your face."

"Okay," Orsea said, and she began to smile. Then, as Adlor began walking up the hill that was behind them, Orsea walked across the field that was in front of her. She sat down on a marble bench under a tall, perfectly straight, stately tree that stood next to a beautiful, blue creek and resumed watching the process that was going on at the Judgement Bar. What she saw intrigued her because to her surprise, even before judgements were announced, as individuals approached the bar, she seemed to know, perhaps by their appearance, the expressions on their faces, what each person's judgement would be.

It was quite disturbing to see how influential Lucifer, and the little devils who had fallen with him from TreLampor, had been while they were on Areth. But it was quite clear that they had been, because there were many, far beyond far too many, of her brothers and sisters who had fallen prey to their enticements. It was such a great heartbreak for her to see how many of Father's and Mother's children had turned against Them and against the Plan of Salvation. For Orsea, it seemed to be nigh impossible to fully comprehend why anyone would make such a choice. And, it was particularly heartbreaking for her to see that amongst those who had lost all opportunity to gain any glory, any glory at all, was Ratack.

Orsea had known Ratack on Areth. Once, they had lived in the same neighborhood and had even worked together, at the same store. She remembered him to be a sweet, kindhearted, jovial person, then. She also recalled that he had actually gained a strong testimony, through the Holy Spirit, of Jesus and of the gospel that He taught. In fact, Ratack, by his own choice, because he knew it was true, had chosen to become a member of Father's church. Orsea had been present at his baptism and was so very happy to know that he had made that choice.

For several years, after their paths had parted, when Ratack's family moved away, Ratack kept in touch with Orsea, and she could tell that he had not only remained a pretty nice guy but had become even nicer. However, and very sadly, things changed way too much! In fact, he changed so much that, after some time, he really was not the same person.

When they ended up in the same place again, because of college, Orsea had quickly been able to see for herself that Ratack was not the person he had been. Apparently, it was so important to him, too important to 'fit in' with others, that he began to make changes. Inappropriate changes in the way he dressed and talked. Soon after that, she saw that his choices of entertainment and recreation were questionable, at best, and were continually becoming more and more horrible as time went on. Before long, Ratack was no longer the person that she had known. He had become an entirely different person and, by his own willful choice, he stayed that way, a way that was not at all good.

He had become so involved in the things of the world, the temporal, mortal world, that Lucifer was able to rule over him. Far too soon, he turned away from the gospel, away from God, away from all that was right and good. In fact, he even spoke out against God, against His church, and against His gospel! He made fun of those who had it, knew its truth, and lived by its principles, precepts, doctrines, and truths.

Orsea had tried many times to bring him back, but he simply would never listen to anything she said.

Orsea tried to teach him what would happen if he continued down the path of apostasy and spiritual anarchy, but that made no difference to him either. In fact, he began to speak out against her, even making some threats. Finally, he just left!

Orsea never knew where he had gone. Numerous times, she had tried to find him, because she never could stop caring about him. But she never did find him. However, seeing him there, in the line for Outer Darkness, she realized that where he went had not been a good place and, sadly, he had never returned to the right side, not even to the least degree.

Now, even though she fully understood that he was getting what he deserved, she was still a bit saddened for him because she knew that he could have done so much better. However, because of the choices that he had made, he would have to spend all eternity in total darkness, true darkness where there would be no light and no glory of any degree. He would experience torment and misery that would be inflicted upon him by his own realization that he, by his choices, had put himself there. And, the only interactions he would have with others would be with Lucifer and his little devils. Oh, and yes, there would be others, like Ratack, who turned against God when they were in the mortal world. They would all have the same, sad fate, forever and ever, and ev... well, you know.

Nonetheless, upside down as it may seem, Ellie was actually grateful that Ratack and the others like him, were not permitted into a kingdom of glory. She knew that they could never endure that, not even the least degree of glory, because they had not lived in such a way as to develop that ability. In fact, that was why she had always referred to them as Heavenly Drop-Outs! They could never again return to Heaven. Still, even though they would not have joy or happiness, at least they would not be destroyed.

Feeling better, with the self-reminder of that realization, Orsea got up, began walking across the field to the far side of the hill and started singing. She had always loved to sing and she knew a bucket-load... no, not just a bucket-load. She had stored in her memory a galaxy-fill of songs. Songs she had learned in TreLampor, songs she had learned on Areth, songs she was learning in StotLampor, songs she wrote, songs... well, you get the idea, lots of songs.

As she approached Paradise Point, she noticed a very large crowd that had gathered just a short distance up from the bottom of the hill. Because her curiosity was never-ending, and even more so because she heard someone cry out, "It is not fair! I should have listened to Orsea." Instead of continuing to... uh... wherever she was going, she began to walk over to the group to see what they were doing, but Micah, the Holy Spirit, stopped her.

"Orsea," Micah, in a soft, pleasant, loving tone, said, "leave them be. Just come here and watch."

Orsea walked over to Micah, stood beside him and did exactly what he told her to do. She watched! And what she saw, though she knew it was for the best, did bring a few tears to her eyes.

Hapnie, who, on Areth, had been a close friend to Orsea from the time they had begun school, at five years of age—Areth age—until they had lost contact with each other in their adult years—Areth years—cried out again, to those who were with her, "I wish I had listened to Orsea! More than anyone else in my life, she tried so many times, in so many ways, always loving and caring, but straightforward too, to teach me not just what I needed to do but why. She always encouraged me to make good decisions. She even corrected me when I did things that I never should have done. Oh, why? Why did I not listen to her?"

As Orsea watched Hapnie slump down to the ground and, with her hands covering her face, cry and cry and cr... oh, you get the idea. As Orsea watched Hapnie cry, she thought back to their time on Areth, remembering that there were times, when Hapnie did behave very well and did make the right choices. That always made Orsea very happy because it testified to her that Hapnie definitely did know the difference between right and wrong.

Because Orsea wanted Hapnie to not only have a good life on Areth, but also to go with her to heaven. The highest degree of heaven, she never stopped talking to her about God's Plan of Salvation. She had tried so hard to get Hapnie to understand that she needed to follow God's directions and live her life the way He would have her do so. She emphasized many times that that was the only way anyone could receive the glory that would bring them the greatest and the most eternal happiness. But Hapnie did not respond well to that because she always wanted to do things her own way.

Sadly, their paths had parted when Hapnie's husband got a job that took them far away. For some time, they did write to each other and even called one another once in a while. But the time came when they lost contact too. While Orsea had hoped, because of what Hapnie had put into some of her letters, that she had been and would be making better choices, the time came when she realized that that would probably not happen.

Hapnie had gotten involved with the wrong kind of friends and she began doing things that were not okay. In college, she cheated on tests and paid other kids to do her homework so she could get good grades. She took things without asking if she could use them, but then she also never returned them. She became such a habitual liar that it got to the point where she really did not even know if what she was saying was true. Not long after she got married and began her family, she also began neglecting them. In fact, she was not true to her husband. And of course, she never owned up to the things that she did, even though she knew they were wrong. That was why, after a while, she had stopped writing to Orsea and broke connections with her. Knowing how important doing what was right and good was to Orsea, and knowing that what she was doing was not, she always felt guilty when they talked, or when she read Orsea's letters.

At that moment, Hapnie stood, faced the brother who was with her, and said, "I know it would have been better for me if I had listened to Orsea and given up the other friends, but I guess, by then, I was already too deep in disobedience. Truthfully, I never got out of it. I never did choose to live by God's laws. I never repented. And now I know, better than I ever did before, why I should have."

As Orsea watched them turn and walk back to the rest of the group, she thought to herself, *I know that Telestial Glory is pleasant and good, far greater than the best of the best that anyone could ever have had on Areth, but it in no way can even begin to compare with the indescribable glory of the higher kingdoms. And sadly, those in the Telestial Kingdom will not be able to be in the presence of our Heavenly Parents and Jehovah. They will only be able to connect with Them through Micah. Still, that is better than no connection at all. At least Micah can visit them and comfort them. And, while they will not be together as families, they will at least be among other people like themselves; they will not be alone and they will not be miserable all of the time. No, what those in the Telestial Kingdom are receiving is not the best that could be had, but it is also not the worst either.*

Still, just as Orsea had felt sad for Ratack, she also felt a bit sad for Hapnie. She realized that Hapnie had at least gotten closer to the greater glory that she could have had. And, she fully understood that, just as Ratack had received all that he could receive, Hapnie had too. While they both could have gotten more, so very much more, Orsea did know that they both got the best that they could because that was all that they enabled themselves to receive and endure.

"Orsea," Micah said gently, "you need to go up the hill. Being here, you are not where you belong!"

After a short pause, knowing full well what Micah meant, Orsea did start up the hill. As she advanced upward, she felt an increasing aura of peace and tranquility wrapping around her. It was a most wonderful feeling, beyond what she had felt at the bottom of the hill, despite all the magnificent beauty that was there. She walked and walked and wal… okay, you know what she did; she walked up the hill, but not all the way to the top. Again, her attention had been captured by another group of people, who, at least from a distance, appeared to be happy.

As she stood quietly, watching their interactions, she could see that, while they were happy. Quite a bit happier than had been those on the lower portion of the hill. There still seemed to be a small melancholy presence among them, a quiet sense of remorse. Now, with curiosity being an eternal trait of hers, Orsea decided that she just had to go over and talk with them. So, over she went.

"Hello," she said to the first person—a man—whom she encountered. When he turned around to see who was behind him, Orsea was startled!

"Veste!" she exclaimed. "What are you doing here?"

While he was not surprised to see her, he was a bit embarrassed. "Hello, Orsea," he replied quietly. "Do you really have to ask that question?"

Now, Orsea knew that she really did not, but she had always hoped that her fears were unfounded. Veste was one of the brothers who had always followed Orsea in TreLampor. She was always teaching the Father's Plan to any and everyone who would listen, and Veste was one of those who did listen. However, Veste had also been one of those who questioned and challenged what was taught.

Oh, and they had also known each other on Areth, not the whole time they were there, but enough of it to have formed a close friendship. So, even though their relationship had ended long before their days on Areth did, because she had known him so well, she never forgot him. Then again, Orsea never forgot anyone. She had wondered if, and hoped that they would go the same kingdom. But now that she was seeing him where she was seeing him, she knew that was not how it would be.

In response to his question, which was not really a question, Orsea finally replied, in a somewhat downtrodden tone, "I guess not really, but I had always hoped…"

When she paused, and knowing that he knew what she was thinking, Veste said, "You always hoped that I would change, repent, and do what I needed to do to get home."

"Yes, Veste," Orsea confirmed, "that is what I hoped."

Then, to her pleasant but sad surprise, he said, "Well, Orsea, I wish I had. I see now what I refused to see or believe then, that I had everything I needed to gain the highest degree of glory, but I could not receive that because I did not fully live according to those guidelines." Then after a short moment of silence, he added, "And, Orsea, I know that this cannot make a difference now, but I am sorry for all the hurt I caused you by not heeding the Father's Plan. You were right. You understood it completely and you lived it. I wish I had."

Veste turned around, walked a short distance up the hill, and joined the rest of the group. As he did so, Orsea watched both his reactions and the group's interactions. They seemed to be happy and, of course, Orsea did know that the glory of the Terrestrial Kingdom was great in its own way. Nonetheless, it still made her a little sad to see Veste with less than the best, less than he could have had. And that was true of everyone who assigned themselves to the Terrestrial Kingdom. After all, these were people who had had the gospel but did not live it fully.

Some of them had not even accepted it when they were on Areth. Though it had been taught to them, they had rejected it. It was not until they left Areth and were in the Post-Mortal Spirit World that they chose to accept the gospel. Those who had received the gospel on Areth did not live by its precepts, principles, doctrines, and commandments with valiance. In fact, Orsea knew that it could very honestly be said that none of them, no matter when they accepted it, had fully lived according to the gospel's doctrines.

So yes, again, as Orsea had felt sorrow for Ratack and Hapnie, she also felt it for Veste. To be so close, but still too far away from the best that could be had, had to be more than just sad.

"At least," she said to herself as she continued her walk up to the top of the hill, "they will be able to be visited by Jehovah, but, sadly, not by Father and Mother.”

Once at the top of the hill, Orsea stopped, stood peacefully still, and looked over the vast expanse before her. It was beyond awesome, indescribably beautiful, magnificently gorgeous, and invitingly peaceful in a way and to the degree that nothing, no nothing! Not anything at all could ever compare to it!

“Oh, my goodness,” she marveled, “I am so beyond grateful that I received the great gift of the Celestial Kingdom!”

“And I am equally grateful that you did,” came a voice from behind her. “But then again, I always knew that you would.”

Orsea turned to see, who she knew that it was, and joyfully exclaimed, “Oh, LePal! I have waited so long to see you again!” Then, giving him a great big hug, which he gladly returned, she added, “You helped me so very, very much, and I could never, even if I knew every language that had ever been created in all the worlds that have ever existed, find enough words to express the fullness of my complete and true gratitude to you! It was rather sad that you could not stay on Areth, with my Daddy; I am certain that you two were the best of buddies in in TreLampor, but I am so happy that you chose to be my Guardian Angel while I was on Areth.”

"Yes," LePal responded, "you are right. HoJes, your Daddy and I have always been very, very close. That was why we were so happy to be able to go to Areth together as twins. Even though I was only there for three days, and your Daddy spent ninrty-five years, four months two weeks, and two days there, we were always together. Oh, and by the way," he added with a hint of celestial humor, "you were right!"

"Right?" Orsea questioned, "Right about what?"

"Well," LePal replied, with a tab bit of an increase in his humor, "when you learned that you had a Guardian Angel, someone who had been assigned to watch over you, you said that our Heavenly Parents knew that taking care of you would be a BIG job, so they chose us, HoJes and me, to be the ones to do just that. HoJes on Areth, as your Daddy, and me from Paradise, as your Guardian Angel. You also added that I had to leave Areth early because I would need a lot of training to look after you!"

"Oh, my goodness!!!!" Orsea exclaimed. "Why do you know that?" Then, after a pause that was too short to even call it a pause, she added, "Oh, never mind. I know why you know that. Nothing about my life on Areth was not known to you because you were always there to see and hear everything."

"Yes, yes I was," LePal said. Then in a loving, tender tone, he quite seriously added, "And I was always very happy with what I saw.

"You did a great job, Orsea. You willing, deliberately chose the right in all things. And when you made mistakes or wrong choices, you voluntarily chose, without hesitation, to correct them and to repent. By choice, your choice, you chose to continually learn the Lord's laws and live by them. And, you unselfishly worked to help others in any and every way you could. Despite the fact that you, for absolutely most of your life felt insignificant, alone, and perfectly imperfect, you never, no never, not once, ever gave up."

With tears of gratitude streaming down her cheeks, Orsea gave LePal a great big hug, which, of course, he returned. Then, just as they were separating from their hug, they heard a voice from before them say, "Hey! I want one of those!" and another voice, from the same direction, add, "I do too!"

Seeing that it was HoJes and Rimai—Orsea's Daddy and Mommy on Areth. Orsea hurried over to them and, while shedding enough tears to create an ocean big enough for Noah's Ark to sail on. Okay, that is a bit of an exaggeration, but you know what I am saying. Anyway, they greeted each other with a mountain of love and happiness.

"Oh, my goodness," Orsea exclaimed, "I am so very, very, ve... well, you know me, so I know you know what I mean; I am so absolutely overjoyed and grateful to see you both!"

"And we are just as delighted to see you," HoJes said, and then added, "and to know that we will now be *together forever*."

"Yes," Rimai concurred, "we are so inexplicably happy, knowing that we all made it and will, indeed, be *together forever*."

"That is what I always wanted, hoped for, and worked for," Orsea added, "to be with my family— families—in the Celestial Kingdom, *together forever*."

For quite some time, they walked and talked. Through the Forever Forest, they shared with one another all that they had learned from many of their experiences on Areth. Over the Peaks of Perfection, they identified the great clarifications and understandings that they had received, when they entered Paradise, about all their mortal experiences. So happy were they to be together again that they shared their feelings with everyone they encountered, until they finally arrived at the Celestial Courtyard, where they were to wait for their turn to visit with Heavenly Father, Heavenly Mother, and Jehovah.

Interestingly though, while everyone, literally everyone who was there, not just at the Courtyard, but in the Celestial Kingdom, was filled with great happiness. Orsea knew that not everyone had received exactly the same degree of that glory nor the same fullness of the opportunities and abilities that it provided. And, be it no surprise, that too brought to her a teeny, tiny, tad bit of sadness. Nonetheless, she was still filled with indescribable joy and happiness to an immeasurable degree for everyone who was there.

She sat down on one of the benches that lined the courtyard and looked around at all who were there. Sitting on a bench that was positioned exactly across from where she was sitting, she saw Rindera, who, on Areth had been one of her distant cousins. Rindera, seeing Orsea, got up and ran across the courtyard to greet her.

"Oh, Orsea," she said with great joy, "I am so happy to see you. I have been waiting for you. I knew you would be here!"

Rising to greet Rindera with a hug, Orsea also said, "And I am so happy to see you here! I love you so much, Rindera; I always have! Sit down, and let us talk a bit."

As Rindera sat down on the bench between Orsea and HoJes, she said, "I have never been happier, Orsea. I could never tell you, when we were on Areth, and I could never express to you here, in SotLampor, how grateful I am that you shared with me Father's

Plan. It made a difference in my life that I never would have imagined anything could. The more I lived it, the more I loved it! When I did things wrong and strove to repent, it always helped me to live even better. Following Father's laws, going to the temple, and honoring the covenants that I made there, is what made it possible for me to obtain the greatest blessing of them all, residence in the Celestial Kingdom! And, Orsea, I want you to know that I did it, not just because I wanted to do what was right, but because I wanted to be where you would be and, as everyone who knew you knew, I knew that this is where you would be!"

"Oh, Rindera, you are so sweet," Orsea replied with loving appreciation.

"But, Orsea," Rindera continued, "I never did get sealed for time and all eternity in the New and Everlasting Order of Matrimony. While, I do admit that that does make me a tad bit sad, I am still inexpressibly grateful to be here, in one of the lower levels of the Celestial Kingdom, rather than just in one of the lower kingdoms. I know that from time to time, we can still interact with one another and that is something I definitely want to do! I also know that, again, from time to time, I will be able to have Heavenly Father, Heavenly Mother, and Jehovah visit with me.

"But there is also another reason I have been so impatiently waiting for you. I want to ask a big favor of you."

"What is it?" Orsea asked curiously.

Taking Orsea's hands in hers, she looked eye-to-eye with her and asked, "Could I please serve you and your eternal companion as a Ministering Angel? I want to be with both of you as often as possible. And, I also want to be of assistance in all the work that you both will be doing as you become a Goddess and he becomes a God."

After a brief, very brief moment of silent thought, Orsea, with true gratitude for Rindera being there in the Celestial Kingdom, lovingly said, "Yes, Rindera, of course. I know we both will be very happy to have you serve for us."

"Oh, thank you, Orsea!" Rindera responded with a ginormous expression of egantic appreciation.

"You are most welcome, Rindera," Orsea replied. "And I want you to know that it makes me feel really wonderful too."

"Now, Orsea, before I go back over to the other side of the courtyard," Rindera said. "I have one more request; will you please sing that little song you wrote about going home?"

"Sure!" was Orsea's unhesitant reply. Then, turning to HoJes, Rimai, and LePal she said, "Because I know that you all know that song too, I am asking you if you will sing it with me."

"Of course!" they all replied in unison, "We would love to!"

"And, Rindera," Orsea said, "you can also join in the singing. In fact," she added, as she looked over the whole group that was in the courtyard, "you all can join in the singing if you would like too. And if you do not know the words, you are more than welcome to hum."

"Thank you, thank you, thank you..." came a universe-fill of replies.

With a feeling of peaceful appreciation for all who were present and all who were not, Orsea began to sing, and everyone else, either with the words or just hums, joined in. Almost as soon as they began singing, a very noticeable sense of serenity encompassed the Courtyard and everyone who was there. To them all, the words of the song held personal meaning.

"Mother and Father, You sent me here because You love me and hold me dear.

"Well, I love You and always will. I'll stand with you on Zion's Hill.

"I'll pray. I'll study. I'll live Thy Laws. And I Will Come Home to You."

"That was beautiful!" Jehovah said as he approached the Courtyard.

"Jehovah!" Orsea exclaimed, with great joy and loving happiness, as she got up, and hurried over to Him, took His hands in hers and then added, "Oh, I am so very happy to see you! It has been a long time."

"Well, only a long Areth time," Jehovah replied with a tinge of teasing, then added, "But yes, I will agree, it has been a long time."

"I missed you," Orsea said quietly.

"I missed you too, Orsea, but We all knew you would be back, and I am so proud of you," Jehovah said to her. "You did everything you committed yourself to do, and you did it all extremely well, despite all the suffering much of it caused you."

"Oh, Jehovah," Orsea said softly but with deep and powerful expression, "compared to what You did for all of us, what You suffered for all, absolutely all of us, my suffering was no suffering at all. Why, that would be like comparing burning in a fire, with a mountain of rocks falling upon you, Your suffering, to breaking a fingernail, my suffering."

"Oh, Orsea," Jehovah chuckled a little, "I love the way you describe things. It is always very depictive but also most entertaining."

After escorting Orsea back to her bench, Jehovah began walking around the Courtyard, speaking to everyone. "You have all done exponentially well," He said. "We are so proud of you and so very pleased and grateful to have you here…" then, looking at Orsea, and with a hint of teasing, He added, "HOME again." Of course, that got smiles and some chuckles from everyone, after which Jehovah continued with, "Father and Mother want each of you to share with Them something of great importance that you experienced on Areth and what, how, and why you learned all that you learned from it. So, it would be good for you to ponder that while you wait to be called up." Then, walking over to Orsea, HoJes, Rimai, and LePal, He said, "You four are first, so come with Me, and I will take you to Them."

As they all walked together, out of the Celestial Courtyard, across the Field of Faith, and down Loyal Lane, Orsea said, "I always knew there would be great joy and happiness in the Celestial Kingdom, but I must admit, during the time I was on Areth, I never could comprehend at least not fully, how great it would be. That Veil of Forgetfulness that was placed over us while we were on Areth sure did work exceptionally well."

"Oh, boy!" HoJes and Rimai said in unison, with emphatic emotion. "That is so true!"

"Well, think not that it was challenging just on Areth," LePal interjected. "Even in Paradise, we did not and could not have a full and completely clear understanding of the greatness of the Celestial Kingdom, or any kingdom."

"That is true," Jehovah added, "and you all know why it was that way, right?"

"Yes," they all, Orsea, HoJes, Rimai, and LePal, replied in unison. "Yes, we do."

"If we had all that knowledge," Orsea said, "we would probably not have needed faith. But without faith, we could not have grown. Without faith, the plan would have been nullified."

"Yes," Jehovah acknowledged, "that is absolutely correct."

They crossed over the Glen of Goodness, passed by the Fountain of Fulfillment, walked through the Golden Gates of Glory, and continued up the Walkway of Worthiness to the Perpetual Palace, where Father and Mother were waiting for them by the Entrance to Eternity.

"Oh, my children," Mother called to them, "come, sit down. We prepared these benches for you."

"Hello, Mother," Orsea said as she gave Her a hug. And then added, "It is so wonderful to be here with You again!"

Then turning to Father, while giving Him a hug, she said, "And, of course it is just as wonderful to be here with You again!"

Both Father and Mother, together, responded with, "Oh, Orsea, We too are so inexpressibly overjoyed to have you HOME!"

After all their greetings were shared, Father and Mother seated them on their benches, with Orsea seated between Jehovah and LePal on her left and HoJes and Rimai on her right. Then Father said, "We want you to share something from your time on Areth that you consider to have been of the greatest importance and most benefit to your progression. We will begin with HoJes, then hear from Rimai, then LePal, and finally, Orsea."

"Well, this is a pretty easy task for me," HoJes began. "I know my life was filled with many struggles, but it was also adorned with many more blessings. Truthfully, I do not believe I would have recognized all the blessings I did receive, or have gained all the knowledge I gained, if I had not experienced all the trials I experienced.

"For example, not by choice, but by command, I had to serve with one of the Armed Forces in World War II. I did not want to do that because not only did I not want to die, I did not want to be the reason anyone else died. And, I had already been saddened by the knowledge that the land of my heritage. The country from which my parents had emigrated was, at that time, one of the enemies of the land of my birth.

"But, when called to duty, I went, and much to my surprise, when I returned home, I did so with gratitude. Yes, I did hear about a lot of horrible things. I did see a lot of devastating occurrences. I did meet a lot of terrible people. But I was also provided with the opportunities to save lives, to make cherished friends, and to come to a greater understanding, that people are not good or bad just because of the country in which they were raised or because of the things they were taught. People, just because they are associated with someone or something that is against what we know to be good and true, are not always aligned with what they are compelled to defend. No, people—all people—are the ones who make their own choices and we need to see the individual as an individual, not as a mere segment of something else.

"Now, with all that said, if no one minds, there is one other thing I would like to share.

"Through Orsea, I was also able to learn that adults, even parents, can learn things. Good and important things from their children. If it had not been for Orsea, I do not believe I would have had the gospel while I was on Areth.

"From her earliest years, doing what Thou, Father, would want her to do, was what she always wanted to do. And that was what led her to the gospel. Your one true gospel that had been restored through Joseph Smith. If it had not been for her devotion and commitment, I doubt the rest of us would have had the gospel in our lives. Learning all that I learned and coming to know all that I came to know, I could never express adequately how grateful I was and am, to have the gospel as my roadmap! Without that, I fear I might not be here today. But because of that, I was able to come HOME!"

"Thank you, HoJes," Mother said. Then to Rimai, she said, "What do you want to share?"

"Well, like HoJes, there are so very many, many things I have to choose from," Rimai began, "but the one that I want to share is this one. Along with Orsea bringing the gospel to us, she always taught us, by her example, not just her words, how to live it. And, she was very good at answering our questions in a way that made sense. This is what I want to share about that.

"After HoJes was taken from Areth, Orsea, because she was so concerned about my well-being, took me to live with her. That, in and of itself, was a wonderful blessing. I did not have to be alone and I did not have to take care of myself, which I could not have done then.

"While there are so many things I could share, the one that stands out as being, at least, one of the most important experiences, occurred sometime in the last year of my life.

"I said personal prayers, but I never would say Family Prayers, Mealtime Prayers, or any prayers in church meetings. I simply would never pray when there was anyone but me present. Many years before that, when I was still pretty new in Thy church, I was offering a prayer with others present, and someone laughed. Even though I never knew exactly what made that person laugh, I felt so embarrassed that I just never could say another prayer unless I was alone.

"Although, Orsea never made me feel bad about that, I knew how important she knew that it was for us to always be willing to offer whatever prayer needed to be offered. So, one day, I asked her if she thought that what I was doing, not being willing to say Mealtime Prayers or Family Prayers, was wrong. It was her response that turned me around, softened my heart, and brought me back to where I should always have been.

"She said to me, 'Well, Mom, let me ask you a question. You said that your other children never call you. One does, once in a while. Another does, but talks to me instead of you. And the other simply never calls at all.' Then she asked me, 'How does that make you feel?'

"I did not need to think about that; I was able to promptly tell her that it made me feel like they did not love me or care about me. That was when she said something that made all the difference. She said, 'Well, Mommy, if you think about prayer as a phone call to Heavenly Father, how do you think He feels when you will not prayer?'

"I do not know if I could adequately describe what I felt after that, but I can tell you that I could not get that question out of my mind. In fact, it was the reason I chose to resume saying Mealtime Prayers and Family Prayers when called upon to do so. It was also what made me think about other things that I needed to improve upon.

"Now, it was not easy, but I most definitely could identify the difference it made. From that experience, I learned how important it is to always, in all ways, stay connected with Thee, Father, Mother, Jehovah, and Micah, and that praying was one of the best ways to do that! I felt so very much better after that, and I was able to feel confident that I would return HOME!"

"Thank you, Rimai," Father said. Then turning to LePal, he said, "What can you share?"

"Oh, Father," LePal began with a tone of teasing in his voice, "if I were to try to share all that I learned from the experiences of Orsea's life, we would be sitting here until the all of the universes collapsed and existence not longer existed."

Naturally, after a statement like that, there was a bit, actually quite a bit, of laughter that occurred. When Orsea was able to stop laughing enough to talk, she asked, "What do you mean by that?"

"You mean you do not know?" LePal asked with another tinge of teasing in his voice, then continued with, "Orsea, watching over you was more than a full-time experience. I learned very quickly why you needed a Guardian Angel."

"Oh, yeah!" Orsea said, with defensive emotion, "Why?"

"Because," LePal responded, and as he did, his vocal tone changed from a tune of teasing to a tone of admiration, "your life was so completely full of trials, trials that were seldom visible to anyone else. Yet, you never, and I do mean never, blamed anyone for your hardships, threw away your belief and trust in God, or gave up. No, never!

"And, despite the fact that you often felt insignificant, unnoticed, no one of any importance, you still reached out to others, caring about them, wanting to be helpful. In fact, if you were ever going to blame anyone for anything, it was always yourself whom you blamed, but not to your demise. Instead, you chose to learn from every challenging situation that you encountered. You chose to take away all the good and the learning from not just your own experiences, but those of others as well, even others who tried to hurt you.

"Father, Mother, Jehovah, what I want to share is this. Having been given the blessed opportunity to serve as Orsea's Guardian Angel gave me the opportunity to learn, to see, what a true follower of

Jehovah is really like. When she did things that she should not have done, she repented sincerely. When she made mistakes involuntarily, she owned up to them and made the corrections. When she received Thy true gospel and even before she had it, she adhered to the truth. She molded her life to it rather than molding it to her life. There is no greater lesson that anyone could learn than that!"

As one might readily expect, true silence followed LePal's comments. It was quite apparent to Father and Mother that LePal had actually received great knowledge and blessings from his service. After a few moments of silence, it was Orsea's turn to share her thoughts.

"Wow!" Orsea said softly. "After all that has been shared, I do not know what to say. I most definitely do agree that life was quite challenging and I will honestly confess that I was not perfect. I know that I took a lot of knowledge and abilities with me when I left TreLampor. But I also know, that because of my imperfections and the trials they caused while I was on Areth, I gained so very much while there! Truly, I came to understand, even before I knew what it was that I understood, how important our mortal lives were and how vitally valuable Thy gospel is, for it is the only true Plan of Salvation, the only accurate roadmap back to here, from whence we came.

"I always looked up to Thee Father, Mother, Jehovah, and to Heaven, because I knew **that is where home is**, and that is where I want to be, eternally."

I Will Come Home

ABOUT THE AUTHOR

Eileen DiStasio-Clark is the second oldest of four children. She is the mother of eleven children and grandmother to twenty-three grandchildren, to date. As a member of The Church of Jesus Christ of Latter-Day Saints, she serves in various positions, teaching, leading, and ministering to children, youth, and adults. Currently, she is also a Family History Missionary. Eileen established the Pursuit of Excellence Institute of Family Education, a non-profit organization focused on strengthening the family. Presently she holds an A.A., a B.A., and an M.A. in Clinical Psychology and is working on the completion of her Doctoral Degree.